Punky Goes Fishing

by SALLY G. WARD

DUTTON CHILDREN'S BOOKS NEW YORK

Published in the United States by
Dutton Children's Books,
a division of Penguin Books USA Inc.

Printed in Hong Kong by South China Printing Co.
First Edition 10 9 8 7 6 5 4 3 2 1

Library of Congress Cataloging-in-Publication Data

Ward, Sally G.
Punky goes fishing/by Sally G. Ward.—1st ed.
p. cm.
Summary: A little girl spends the day fishing with her grandfather.
ISBN 0-525-44681-8
[1. Fishing—Fiction. 2. Grandfathers—Fiction.]
I. Title.
PZ7.W2158Pr 1991
[E]—dc20 90-35538 CIP AC

for Jonathan

Punky was sleeping over at her grandparents' house.

"Grampy," she asked, "may I go fishing with you tomorrow?"

"Well, Punky," said Grampy, "let me think about it. Fishing is serious business, you know."

The next morning, Punky had just finished her breakfast when Grampy surprised her. "What do you say, Punky . . . want to try some fishing?"

So they prepared
their lunches,

and Punky put on her old clothes.
"I'm bringing a towel, in case you get
wet," said Grampy.

Grampy gave Punky a little fishing pole.
"It's just the right size for you, Punky,"
he said. "And here's my great big one for
catching the big fish."

“I want you to wear this life jacket, dear,
so Grampy knows you’re safe.”
“Don’t you need to wear one, Grampy?”
asked Punky.
“Oh no,” Grampy laughed. “I never fall in.”

Out on the water, Punky watched the houses get smaller.
"It's so quiet out here, Grampy," she said.
"That's why I like it," Grampy replied.

"And here's where we stop, Punky.
The water is only up to my middle.
Plenty safe. I'll set the anchor."

The anchor went in easily.
But so did Grampy's lunch.

“That’s all right, Grampy. You can share mine.”
“Thank you, Punky,” said Grampy.

Grampy got the poles ready,
and they sat back to wait.

"Any nibbles yet, Grampy?"
"Nope . . . well,
wait a minute. . . ."

"Wow, Grampy. You caught a teeny one."
"Yup," he said, "that one goes right back in."

The fish went in easily.

But so did one of the oars.

"Good thing I brought my waders," said Grampy. "When we're done, I'll *pull* us back to shore."

"I'm hungry, Grampy. Let's have lunch."
"Good idea, Punky. I'm hungry, too."

After lunch Grampy said, "Let's try one more time, all right?"
"Sure," said Punky. "Only, can I fix my own hook? I want to try a little piece of the leftover fig bar on it."

“Ha ha,” laughed Grampy. “Never heard of a fish who wanted to take a bite of a fig bar.”

"Take it from me. Your old grandpa knows what's what. Especially when it comes to fishing."

"Grampy! I think I've got something!"

"GRAMPY! I *know* I've got something!"

"Keep reeling, Punky. I'm coming."

"Looks like
a whopper!
GOTCHA!"

The fish stayed in the net.
But Grampy went over.

"Wow, Grampy! Wait till Grammy sees what I caught."

It was time to go home.

"Grampy! You got a fish, too!
Can we go again tomorrow?"